THE GOLDEN SEED

BY
MARIA KONOPNICKA

ADAPTED BY
CATHARINE FOURNIER

ILLUSTRATED BY JANINA DOMANSKA

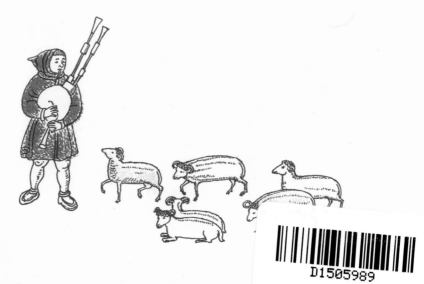

CHARLES SCRIBNER'S SONS

NEW YORK

A long, long time ago there was a King who ruled over a faraway country beyond the mountains.

It was a happy and a peaceful land.

Every morning the birds and the children woke the King with their sweet singing. And every morning the King thought:

"My country is rich in the beauties of nature.

"The sky is full of singing birds. When one flies away, another comes.

"The meadows are full of flowers. When one fades, another blooms.

"There are red apples and yellow pears in the orchards.

"There is game in the forests.

"There are fish in the rivers.

"We have horses and sheep and cows."

But there was one thing the country did not have—
and that was gold. This made the King very sad, for every
morning he thought, too, of his people. They worked from
dawn to dark. Their food was plain, their clothing rough.
Many country people wore the skins of animals, and many
children in the towns had never seen a real shirt.

"If only," wished the King, "if only there were gold
in my kingdom.

"I would dig it out of the earth.

"I would send it to faraway countries.

"I would buy clothing for my people.

"Everyone will trade for gold."

Then he sighed a great sigh and pulled at his mustache.

"If only," he wished again, "if only there were gold in my land."

One day in early spring when the King was out walking, he met some merchants riding along on their camels. The King was surprised to see them, for few merchants visited his country. The merchants, in turn, were astonished to see a king walking along a lonely road. They stopped and began to show him the things they had to sell.

The King felt soft furs, he gazed at his reflection in bright mirrors, he smelled perfumes and spices. But nothing interested him.

"There is only one thing I wish for," he said to the merchants, "to find gold in my land so my people will not be poor."

The merchants looked at each other. They could not grant such a wish. But among them was a wise old man, dressed in white, with silvery hair and a long silvery beard. He understood the King's wish.

"O King," he said, "I have here a bag of seed. If you sow this seed in the ground in the springtime, it will flourish and grow into gold." He took from his saddlebag a large sack which he opened and set before the King. The sack was full of smooth, greenish-brown seeds.

Seeds which would grow into gold! The King was overjoyed. Here was the answer to his wish. He took the sack, and in exchange he gave the old merchant his great royal ring.

Although the bag of seed was heavy, the King carried it back to the castle himself.

The next day heralds announced to the people that a
month hence the King himself would sow a seed in the
ground which would grow into gold.

The air grew warmer and the earth softer. The time
of planting had come. Mothers brought their babies,
and young men brought their fathers. There was a huge
crowd, for everyone wanted to see the marvelous sowing.

The King wore his crown and his finest robes and rode upon his tall gray horse. With him were all his court and his heralds and musicians. The King's Treasurer carried the bag of seed under a crimson canopy.

When they came to the field, the musicians played
and the heralds sounded their trumpets. The King re-
moved his crown. Then, like a simple farmer, he walked
along the freshly plowed furrows, scattering the seed in
the moist soil. The greatest lords of the land walked
behind him and covered the seed with the rich black
earth.

When the seed was sown and covered over, the King put his crown on his head, mounted his gray horse, and led a happy procession back to the castle.

"Now," he thought, "I have a field sown with gold!" And there was joy in his heart. At last he was doing something for his people.

Each morning the King looked out his castle window to see if the gold was growing.

One day there was a warm rain and when the sun came out, the King saw hundreds of tiny green shoots pushing up through the earth. He was so happy that he did a little dance.

"Next year," he said, "I will sow a field ten times bigger!"

And he promised himself that he wouldn't look at the field again until the little green shoots had a chance to turn their true golden color.

A week went by, and he could wait no longer. He looked again. He was surprised to see, not the yellow of gold, but the rich green of a thousand growing plants.

He pulled at his mustache and wondered why the gold did not show.

He waited another week and then another. Now there was an army of little green stalks in the field. Everyone who passed thought, "How can gold come from a common plant?"

The King's courtiers shook their heads and whispered in the great hall. But the King was not worried.

"There is nothing wrong," he told everyone. "When the flowers come, they will surely be gold."

One morning the King looked out his
window and saw the field covered with flowers as blue
as the sky. Then he began to worry. He couldn't eat his
supper and he went to bed troubled. But in the morning,

when the birds and the children woke him,
he slapped his forehead and cried:

"How stupid I am! Of course the *seed*
will be gold, not the flowers."

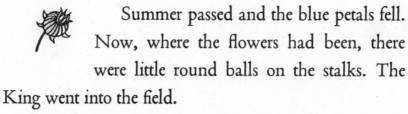 Summer passed and the blue petals fell. Now, where the flowers had been, there were little round balls on the stalks. The King went into the field.

"Surely," he thought, "the gold is in these little balls."

He reached out and picked one from its stalk.

"If I just break this ball, gold will spill out on the ground."

Slowly he closed his hand and crushed the little pod. But when he opened his fingers, he saw only the same greenish-brown seeds he had sown in the spring.

Now the King was angry indeed. He
ordered his men to pull up the plants, beat
them with sticks, and throw them into the
river. He was terribly disappointed. And he was ashamed
of himself. How could he have been foolish enough to

believe that gold could grow from an ordinary seed?

He commanded his men to search all through the kingdom for the old merchant who had dared to cheat him. And once more the King grew sad, for he knew that his people were no better off than they used to be.

One day when he was walking near the
river, he saw something ın the water held down by large
stones. He told one of his men to go into the water and
find out what lay there. When the man returned, he told
the King:

"Sire, it is that weed which was supposed to grow
into gold."

The King scowled. "Must I be reminded how foolish I was?" he cried. "Take the weeds out of the river and out of my sight!"

So the King's men waded into the river, lifted the heavy stones, and pulled up the rotting stalks. They carried them into the forest and threw them on the ground.

Now the King was very unhappy, and his lords wished to cheer him. They decided to arrange a great hunt. All the noblemen of the kingdom were invited. They came with their horses and dogs and falcons, with their bows and arrows and spears and pikes.

It was the biggest hunt that had ever been seen in the land.

In the excitement the King *did* forget his unhappiness. When everything was ready, he mounted his gray horse and led the hunters off to the great forest. The horns blew, the dogs barked, the horses neighed, and the falcons screamed—as big and happy a noise as you could imagine.

 But no sooner were they in the forest than the King saw the bundles of weeds which his men had thrown there. His happiness turned to anger. He ordered the hunt to stop. All his enjoyment vanished. In a black mood, he rode home.

When he reached the castle he was still angry. He ordered his men to thrash the weeds to shreds. The men returned to the forest. They beat the stalks so hard with

sticks there was nothing left but pale shreds of fiber. Then
they threw the mangled stalks upon the crossroads, for
the sun to burn and the wind to blow away.

And still the King's men searched for the old
merchant.

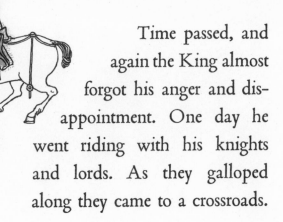

Time passed, and again the King almost forgot his anger and disappointment. One day he went riding with his knights and lords. As they galloped along they came to a crossroads.

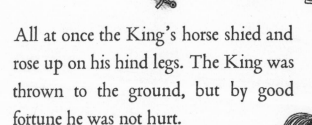

All at once the King's horse shied and rose up on his hind legs. The King was thrown to the ground, but by good fortune he was not hurt.

The knights dismounted to see what had frightened the King's

horse. They saw the shredded stalks strewn in the crossroads. The King had been pale with fright, but now he grew red with anger. He ordered his servants to beat the stalks again, and this time to burn them.

Just as they were about to set fire to the silvery fibers, a messenger rode up to the King.

"Sire," he cried, "we have found the old merchant!"

At once the King rode back to the castle. The guards brought in the old man bound with ropes. The King

looked so angry that the court hardly dared to breathe. Only the old man did not seem frightened. Walking up to the King, he said quietly:

"Sire, you had me hunted as a thief. Here I am. But I was coming to you of my own free will for I knew you needed me. Sire, let me speak to you alone."

The King was furious. "I shall throw you into prison," he shouted, "for you cheated me! You told me the seed would grow into gold. It grew into a weed!"

"Put me in prison if you will, Sire," the old man replied, "but let the weed go to prison with me."

To this the King agreed, and the old man and the heap of fibers were thrown into prison.

Now the prison keeper had a daughter whose name was Rose. She was as kind as she was beautiful, and she grew to love the old man, who told her stories of the great world beyond the mountains. When she brought his food to the cell, she would also bring her spinning wheel. As she spun coarse wool for a shepherd's coat, the old man busied himself combing the silvery fibers of his weeds.

One day he asked Rose to spin thread
from the shreds of the plant which he had
combed out so carefully. Rose did as he
asked.

"Now take the thread home, Rose," he
said, "and weave it into cloth."

Again she did as he asked. She stretched
the threads on her loom and wove and wove. As
she worked, a fine, soft cloth began to appear.

When she had used all the thread, Rose
brought the cloth to the old man.

That very day a messenger from the King came to the prison to see the old merchant.

"Ask whatever you will, old man," the messenger said, "for today the King's daughter is to be married, and the King would show mercy to all."

"I would like to give the Princess a gift," the old

man said. "I beg you to take me to the King."

Still in his prison chains, the old merchant was led from the dungeon and brought before the King. A great crowd of guests filled the castle hall, and in their midst stood the Princess, lovely as a lily, and her bridegroom, handsome as the sun.

When the King saw the old man, he scowled, but on this day he could not be angry. He asked the old man what he wished.

"Sire," said the merchant, "I bring a gift for the Princess."

And he spread out before the King the fine snow-white cloth that Rose had woven and bleached in the dew and sun.

The King marveled at its softness.

"What is this cloth?" he asked.

"This, O King," replied the old man, "is linen, the gold from the seed I gave you. My seed is FLAX, the riches of the poor. All the things you did to the plant were good for it, because flax must be soaked, and then dried, and then beaten again and again. Even what you did to me was good, for a kind child took care of me in prison, and I taught her to spin the flax and to make the linen.

"But, Sire, it was not good to do these things in anger, without understanding or mercy."

And turning to the Princess, the old man said:

"Gentle lady, please take my gift. Then ask your
father, the King, to sow flax again and to treat it as before,
but this time with love. The linen cloth your people weave
will serve your land better than gold."

The King was heartily ashamed that he had treated the merchant so unjustly. He stood up and put his arms around him.

"Old man," he said, "I thank you, for you have done what I could not do. I wished for gold, but you gave me something better. Now my people will go dressed in linen."

Then the Princess decreed that the old man's gift should be made into shirts for the children.

And there was great joy in all the kingdom.